# WHAT iF, Pig?

## Linzie Hunter

HARPER

*An Imprint of HarperCollinsPublishers*

What If, Pig?

ISBN 978-0-06-298609-2

The artist used Procreate and Photoshop to create the digital illustrations for this book.
Design by Linzie Hunter and Chelsea C. Donaldson
21 22 23 24 25   RTLO   10 9 8 7 6 5 4 3 2 1

First Edition

What if you had a friend like Pig?

What if he was the nicest pig you'd ever met?

What if he was incredibly **KIND,**

fabulously **FUN,**

and endlessly **GENEROUS?**

But it's your favorite!

What if you felt pretty lucky
to have a friend like Pig?

That's how Mouse felt.

In fact,

that's how everyone felt

about Pig.

Pig was so kind
and so generous
and so much Fun
that he had a brilliant idea.

**W**hat
if I throw
a party?

# PARTY CHECKLIST

☑ hats

☑ decorations

☐ snacks on sticks
**NO** SAUSAGES

☐ cake ~~or~~ AND
donuts

☑ make invitations
↑
FANCY

☐ top tunes

☐ games
PRIZES FOR ALL!

JACK

RSVP

ma

Pig's party was sure to be the talk of the town.

Doggo

the Bunny Bros.

BeaR

CAt

Ms. Petunia

Squirrel

Vera

Uncle Potato

Duck

William

Ollie

Bob

C.K.

TRevok

IRIS

mail

Professor
Waffles

Pogi

Boris

Satomi

Lotta

But
what if
Pig
had a
Secret?

Pig was a **TREMENDOUS WORRIER.**

A **PORKY Panicker!**

A **Proper Nervous Nelly.**

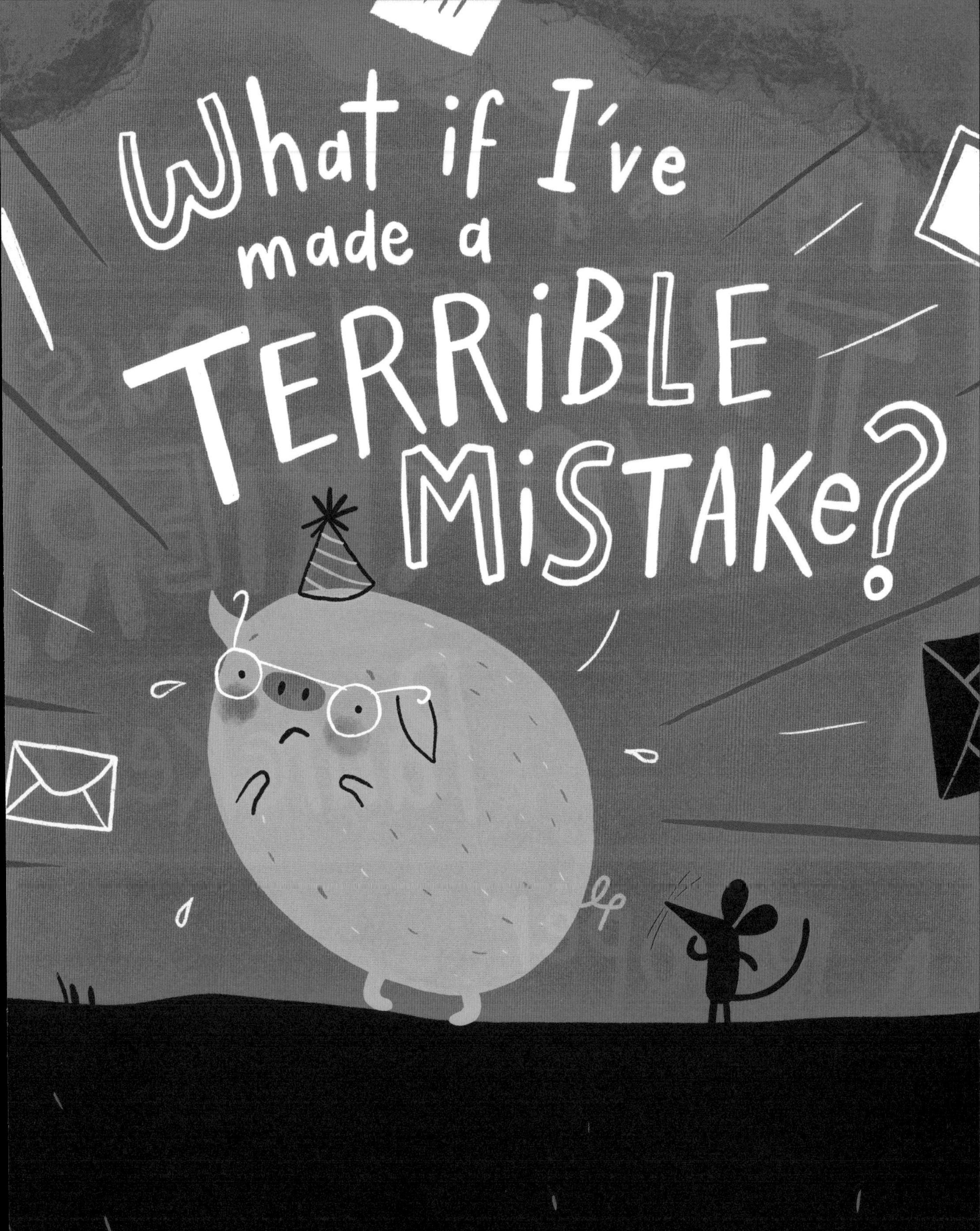
What if I've made a TERRIBLE MISTAKE?

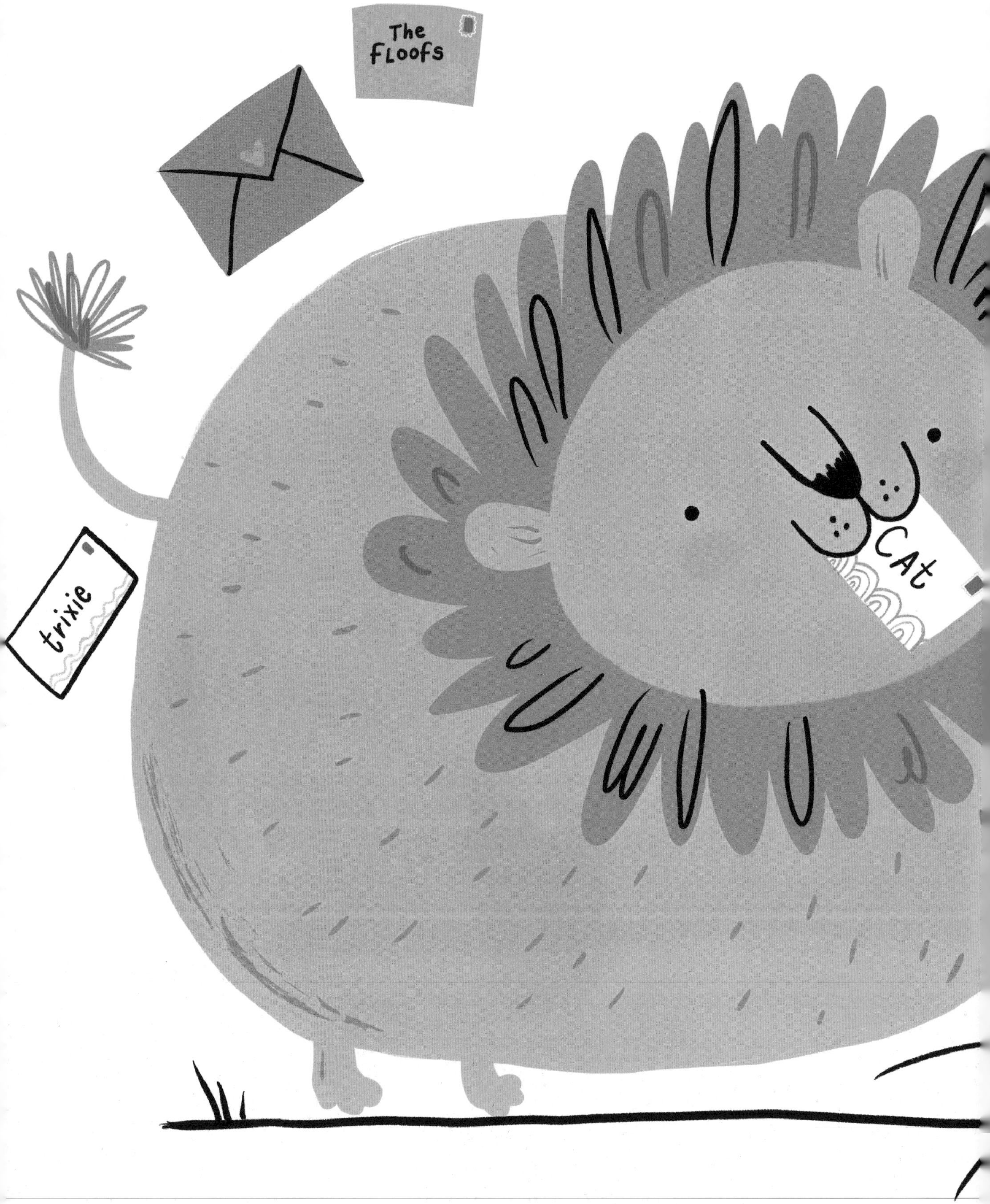
The FLoofs
trixie
CAt

# What if a FEROCIOUS LION eats all the invitations? Or worse...

ORIN

the Bunny Bros.

mail

# EATS
## all the guests?!

# What if everyone gets stuck in a MASSIVE BLIZZARD?!

What if nobody comes?

Or Worse...

and has an absolutely **AWFUL** time?

Trevor had a chocolate fountain.

And an ice sculpture.

What if... What if... What if... What if... What if... What if... What if... What if... What if... What if... What if... What if... What if... What if... What if...

What if... What if... What if... What if...

What if . . . no one
really likes me at all?

I know—
What if I Cancel the Party...

tell everyone
I'm sick,

go to bed,

and never leave
the house?

Okay, Pig,
if you're
sure.

What if we go for a little walk?

Mouse, what if I

always

feel

sad

?

Don't worry, Pig . . .

Things don't stay
gray for very long.

What if we all talked about our worries?

I'm slow.

I'm not even outdoorsy!

I get really nervous around cats.

Me too.

Mousie! Yay!

Mouse,
what if I have the kindest,
most generous

and fun friends
a pig could meet?

Yes, Pig,
what if?